Songs Of Hills

Lovers to Strangers

Nisha Lamichaney

Ukiyoto Publishing

For Late Rupa Lama, always in our heart

Acknowledgement

To my mother and my friends for persuading me to publish this book. Gratitude to my editor Biswa for all the effort he put in embellishing my work and my graphic designer Sawrav for his sensitive designs.A special thank you to my husband Bikram for always being a great motivator in my life.

Contents

Introduction

Not with the intention to publish rather to quietly capture the 'spontaneous overflow of emotion'triggered by relationships with people, places and the past that this collection of poems had been written over a course of several years.

Yielding to the persuasion of friends, who had read the verses that this otherwise personal penning is now made available to all who have an interest in poetry.

Songs of Hills consists mostly free verses but are harmonized with a narrative, an ode, an elegy and a couplet. Transitioning from one verse to another are a dozen haikus – a comic relief between spells of seriousness if you will.

The 'editing' of the poem has been limited to language, form and structure, much like dressing a bride for her wedding. To fully appreciate the mood and moral of the poems, the editor and poet spent over a year 'embellishing' the verses before sending it to the press.

The visual insertions are pictorial interpretations and illustrations of some of the poems. While the pictures are mainly for aesthetic purposes, each of them is intrinsically woven into the fabric of this anthology

Pause

Stop,

*Open your eyes to the pouring of this poet's heart, Before
starfish nibble her words, add to your cart.*

Look,

*Bathe in the balm of the winter sun, Watch the yellow
swallowtails flitter in fun.*

*Pause to spectate the dreamy clouds change colour, Fluffy balls
of milky white in a sea of lucid lavender.*

Pause and observe the smoke like mist,

Rising from the forest and blue hills it kissed.

Walk,

*Breathe in the floating forest musk, Pine needles, dry cones sans
your mask.*

*Pause and examine the hollow footprints, Crushed snow, some
grumpy boots it hints.*

Pause and gaze at the floating specks of light, A sheet of dense fog, diffusing through the night.

Listen,

Tune in to the sound of the rolling brook, Beating a rhythm, cascading down the nook.

Pause and surrender to the moon, gleam and glow, Chaperoned by the band of amorphous constellation.

Pause and awaken to the ominous silence,

The hooting owl, the crying fox in sinister alliance.

Meditate,

Breathe in the saccharine flavours of the season, Close your eyes to this illusionary vision.

Puddles, potholes,
Bubbles of sloshing water,
Floating paper boats!

A long and winding road

A long winding road, Barren and bald, Weathered and trampled

By souls striding back and forth.

The ebb and flow

Of red robes sweeping the ground, the wrinkled faces,

The monastic decree.

Chants of wisdom, Strings of beads

Around which their fingers dance in meditative rhythm.

Beyond human civility, Beyond the blurry horizon Is sewn in fabric of greens,

The earth sprouting with vitality.

Beams of the golden sun

Tan trees, transfer tones and textures to the landscape around me.

A heavenly tapestry.

Up there, a whistling thrust, tweets from the tree tops (Calling
its love, perhaps)

On a sunny afternoon, a quiet visitor,
Ruffles the leaves,
On the long winding road.

Cold sheet of earth beneath, shiny crown of tree above, blanket
of green around, he drowns in silence.

A string of prayer flags, Tied to the tree tops.
Dances under the beams of sunlight like humming bird.

The silent visitor looks up
at the diamonds on the crown.
The mighty monarch of the mountains, casting long shadows on
the road.

The visitor halted his gait and twitched his head.
The mist then slowly lifted To reveal a white Stupa
(A manifestation of the cosmos)
At the far end of the long winding road.

His hunger satiated,
His thirst quenched,
His eyes closed,
His hands folded,
His body bowed,
To the holy abode.

Such was the story told
By a lonely visitor,
Who walked the long winding road.

Clear blue autumn sky,
Wreaths of marigold plenty,
Deep fried selroti!

Blowing in the wind

A mottled feather,
Moulted and set free, Ascends, descends
Through uncertainty.

Impelled by the gale, Swaying in its gushy trail, Tosses, turns
and
Resists the winds of God.

On Earth this humanity,
Is a floating feather, Gliding through time,
Blowing in the wind.

Is this our sanity,
To swim against the tide
To kick air for new direction,
For the grass on the other side?

Our body weighs us down, Drops as breezes die.

Our soul seeks to fly,

But broken wings can only cry.

This mottled feather, Buoyantly hugging the air, As consorts to the Gods, Has wisdom to share.

Our lives knitted in pieces, By the delicate weft of destiny, So charmed, spelled we live, Aligned by stars in our galaxy.

Paddling across this ocean of obscurity, Shall we learn to live?

This mottled feather is us; Resist the strong gush, Ascend, descend,

Hold equipoise, stay afloat.

A serpentine road,
A car slithering uphill,
A bored passenger!

Cherry Blossom

A flushed glow of spring sets in. Sweet aroma lingers in the air.
Petite petals stretch their limbs, freed From the clutches of crude
winter.

Ice flakes melt on the ground. The earth lies moist with life.
Frail forms rise from repose,

Crawling, they make their way out.

My eyes pan the rolling horizon, Snow clad peaks in the
distance, Meet her standing splendidly serene, In a chanced
encounter.

There she stood poised and firm Under the velvety blue sky.

I locked my gaze to flirt,

With the beauty, with the cherry tree.

The silhouette of her body; Upright in all its gracefulness;
Soaked in a vicarious pleasure; Her leaves swaying in the wind.

Her bosom covered by,
A knitted embroidery of pink.
A festoon of flowers Hung carelessly and flushed With the
colors of rouge.

Oh Cherry! My beautiful Cherry, Your blossom enthralls my
mind. Like a blessing on a scourge, you heal my wounded
heart.

As I sit under your refuge, my mind consumed by a
"Fear of Impermanence".
A wave of nostalgia rises and lashes the shores of my heart.

My dear Cherry!
(I say out loud.)
How bravely you face it all.
A rebel to the raging seasons, You defy the perilous frost.

As nature spins its yarn,
Sets Kala Chakra in motion,
The perilous frost retreats
And takes with it her colour,
Her petals,I bid Her adieu.

Months later, I hear a knock. It's Spring come a calling!
Sweet aroma lingers in the air, Delicate petals smile and blush,
My beautiful Sakura blossoms again!

Glimpse of rugged hills,
Sheet of snow over Tsomgo,
Screams of ecstasy!

Dreamweaver

A dream I weave inside my mind,
Tortuous thoughts, fantasy run wild.
Trembling hands thread slow but steadily,
Loosening here and stiffening there,
Pulling pieces of what's left to spare.

All I see is you and me,
Dancing away most gleefully.
Worries, sorrows tossed to the sea.
That's the only glimmer in this dark,
A light I follow with a pounding heart.

Tomorrow is yet another journey,
Yesterday left a scary scar behind.
Now I want our love to shine.
This life stalled in salty doldrums,
Waits for a wind while life benumbs.

This reverie is all I hold on to,
Dancing away most gleefully.
Worries, sorrows tossed to the sea,
Sailing through the sands of time,
Forever till the end of the line.

A patlinukkad,
Brick walls stained in graffiti,
Smell of ammonia!.

Free spirit

Hymns of devotion
Pierce the realm of imagination.
Prayer flags flutter,
Scriptures scatter,
Harmony hovers,
Over deluded minds.

This world
Of morbid realities,
Tied together,
By the leash of time,
Tempts the soul.
And so we succumb,
And so we sink,
Deep into
The slushy sand
Of time.

The search for salvation
Is but a question of refuge.
Do we hang on to the strings of spirituality?
Dive into the Ganges,
Climb to the summit of Enlightenment,
Levitate in the thin air of reality?
How do we,
Set our spirits free?

Reed hands, iron wheels,
Squeeze the life out of rattans,
Roadside sugar rush!

Rendezvous with the moon

On a cool lonely night
The moon and I
Played hide and seek.
Peekaboo! I see you.

As it glided across the sky,
Hiding behind quilts of white cloud,
It lit up the fluffy balls of cotton,
A halo in the heavenly garden.

And the night slipped by,
The constellations like a burst of fireflies
Shone to brighten our play,
Twinkled in a cheerful display.

Now the silhouette of the jagged horizon,
Echoed with the applause of crickets.
Dark trees and shady shrubs
Waved their leafy flags at us.

As the cool draft of wind,
Caressed my face and ruffled my hair,
It was long past midnight,
But the moon was a beautiful sight.

Relentless knife hacks
Tough green head with hidden smile,
A straw to drink it!

Devil beats the drum

Dire thoughts in all its fury,
Raise hell and sets ablaze,
The land of the Nod.
Cold as carcass,
Tossed to the vultures,
The Temple lies frozen,
In the dead of the night.

In the masquerade of life,
She'd fashioned a grand entry.
Warning bells from rooftops cried
But deaf to her,
The disaster in disguise.
The Temple unsanctified.
Now lies in a state so dreary.
Chaos! A fetid potpourri.

In the darkest of nights,
In the deepest of sleep,

The devil beats the drum:
Lashing, gashing, hammer and tong
Tearing the Temple on a song.
This battered body sweats and melts,
Laid bare on the anvil of anxiety.

Was it a nightingale?
that Sang tales of a tryst,
Perched on the Alder tree?
For a call came in
From deep within,
Hankering me back to reality.

A familiar voice called my name,
Warm words seasoned the air.
An angelic choir of a church
Tuning the Temple's discordant affair.

"Worry not over worldly woes,"
Comforted the gentle spirit.
Cassiel hummed me a lullaby

Pouring potion so sweet,
Carrying me off to sleep.
The devil beat a retreat in haste,
His shouts melted like snowflakes.
On a lifeless winter bed when
Left to the mercy of the Sun.

Rivers of joy, warmth and life,
Tributaries on my desert face.
As she beamed over my soul,
This Temple embraced in her fold.

A pair of myna,
Pecking trash on the sidewalk,
Two rupee good luck!

Glorified love

I came across a Garden of Gods.
A paradise of pleasure
Ruled by the Spirit of Love.
Dancing and twirling
Dewy tendrils so tender,
The holy aspergillum
Sprinkling Stardust
Mystical portions
Casting spells.

The Spirit sublime,
Shifting shapes,
Dazzling my eyes,
Gestured me into her world.
Yielding to the glow,
Like innocent petals of a rose,
My heart bloomed again.

Radiating brilliance,
The Kohinoor,
Blinded me.
On the spotlight,
The prime donna,
Hit a crescendo,
Emotions erupted,
Molten magma from the core.

Then curtain fell,
The spells unspelled,
Paradise lost,
The Garden of Gods,
Unweeded, infested.

Into a wailing wilderness
I'd sleepwalked,
Feet blistered,
Emotions emptied,
Picking up memories,
Dead flowers,
Dry twigs,

Scraping the dust.
And so this Glorified love,
Withered and smothered.
But when spring shines
Roses bloom,
And so this foolish heart
Sleepwalks to the Garden of the Gods,
Falls prey to the Spirit of Love,
Like innocent petals of a rose,
Yielding to the glow, yet again.

Like a phoenix from its ashes,
In an evanescence of emotions,
Defies the fire of its past,
I rise again,
To tell the tale
Of glorified love.
A prodigy of existence!

Early morning sight
Empty basket and gumboots,
An ominous sight!

The hills never sleep

A glimmer in the dark, a low gargling tune,
It's the cold water caressing Teesta's dune.
Like a sheet of silk hung out to dry
flapping and clapping to the wind's cry.

The Teesta ripples and pulsates with life
Under the crushing scoops of tide.
Fallen twigs raft hopelessly,
Like forsaken souls endlessly
Drifting in the river of life.

Trees turn shadows now the Sun's dim,
Their majesty bent under the moonlight.
Selena shines, body scarred from the fight.
The wolves howl, the hills grow grim.

As civilization sleeps, the hills hum a song,
ballads of the days long gone.
The ravages of time- their chorus,

The collision of tectonic plates - their crescendo
The building of the dam - their outro.

They also render in sweet verse
The lovers in leisurely traverse,
Who lean under their cool shades,
Hold hands and make promises.

It's in this silent symphony of the hour,
My mind begin to scour
For meaning of life — sweet yet sour.
Somewhere behind the drapes of the night
A soul's tired but sleeps despite.

Somewhere under the blanket of the night
A mother tucks her child tight.

Somewhere under the canopy of the night
Weekend warriors unite.

Somewhere under the shroud of the night,
A heart turns stalactite.

Hanging on despite the strife,
Salty waters dripping of plight,
Somewhere under the shroud of the night.

My sleepless ear echoes,
The river and its sliver,
The hills and their shrills,
The Teesta and its operetta
The lives and their knives
The hills never sleep.
They never let me sleep.

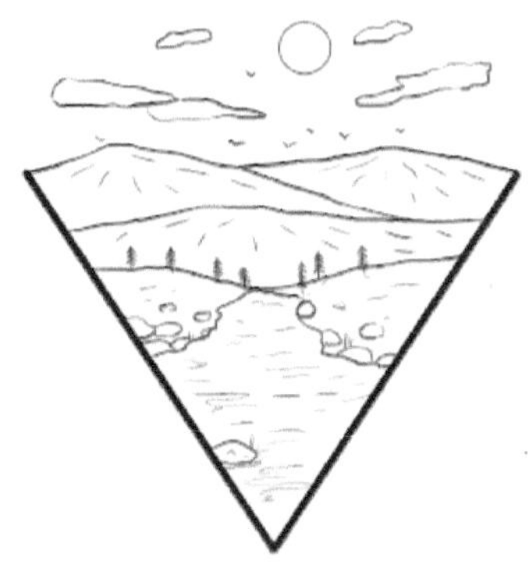

Drizzle in the air,
Raindrops vanish in the ground,
Subtle scent of earth.

The Wilderness

A bamboo grove
Embellished by laces of leaves,
Knife-like, rustled in a raspy whisper
When blown by the breeze.

Beyond lay a paddy field,
Mellowed by the golden sun,
The harvest of the season.
The foliage waved, Come along!

A train of smoke invaded the sky.
Burning wood and upturned earth,
Callous feet and arid hands,
The arduous life of a solitary reaper.

Into the wilderness
My footsteps a tap tap,
Following the sounds of life,
I toddled into nature's lap.

A doll's house!
Out of the blue,
In a green world,
Made me pause.

Sunflowers, tall and bright,
Stood guard beside the window.
But the porch was inviting
And I befriended a stool.

Now birds began to croon.
I commenced to contemplate,
Walk into the wilderness
When the world stops making sense.

The white curtain drawn,
Bright sunlight floods her way in,
Stale sleepy face glows.

Stars in the galaxy

*Blue sweater of the fine cashmere wool, Trimmed tailored pant
with crisp lining,*

*Leather shoe shinning with the slightest ray of sun touching its
surface,*

No grit or grime to tend to.

A faint smile creating new ripples of folds across his face,

Those delicate wrinkles reflecting the signs of happiness,

*Lived in complete satisfaction in all of these ages, His
handsome face brightly lit with an ethereal glow, As he came to
greet us in the early hours of morning Before the morning hauled
us of out the dream.*

Such was the reunion,

*The visit short but the dream so vivid, Yet the moment of
departure was inevitable.*

As I playfully set my heart, On the hard bark of the oak tree,

*The beautiful cones clanking into the ground, Under the
pressure of my hand.*

My body trembled with a sense of delight, In a moment of silence there he was gone, Like the fading mist of the morning,

No sign of his presence whatsoever,

Oh! How he carefully seated himself amongst the stars and watched us from above.

The sound of carouse,
Midnight hour erupts in cheers,
The smell of bonfire.

My dear heart

*Below bedazzling episodes of son et lumière Lie dark stretches
of a heavy heart.*

*Its chambers echo in cold, murky void, Moans the soul from its
shadowy lair*

Icy thoughts flood its nervous hemisphere.

Oh! Dear,

Why don't you lie down in peace?

This isn't your world. Why don't you speak?

Why does your gentle heart weep?

Who is it that you seek?

*You see a life without pain and sorrow, How foolishly to let
false hopes grow!*

*Your desires break all bounds, How like Icarus you've become!
I'd warned you time and again.*

Dear, pull yourself up. Don't you die in vain!

*You are captive of your own fear. Spread your wings and
disappear. Don't let delusions prey your soul, Fly away from
this depressing atoll.*

Muse

Bewitching were his charms, His manner so calm and composed,

A demeanour so enthralling, His nature kind and pure.

So fond she grew of his manners, His sweet gestures stirred her soul,

How beautifully his lips curled to its sides, If only she could savour the sight of it all.

Every day from dusk till dawn, She kept his close to her heart.

His thoughts kept lingering inside her mind in circles, Day in and day out!

Every night, while retiring of to bed, She pondered about her life.

How beautifully those times would be, Spent together by his side.

Yet, by the early hours of dawn, When the birds start to sing,

When the ray of sun kissed her face, She awakened from her dream.

A dream, a dream, a beautiful dream!

So pious is it in every way.

*Alas! The brutal reality sank its fangs in, Like the venomous
snake,*

And sucked the life away!

Shattered and forlorn, She began to weep,

The mirage was long gone, Under the glowing sun!

*Yet, again the ray of hope came alive, Yet, again the heart be so
gently fooled, It cared no other thing but love,*

The taste of the forbidden fruit!

Reverence

As I bow my head,

My hands folded in prayer, As I kneel,

My head touching the gritty stone, My heartbeat flees in fear.

My mind fills with remorse. I drown in a sea of sin.

Emotions erupt.

I tumble through time.

I close my eyes.

And see sacred sanctity.

Faith is fortified. Tomorrow is mine. Emotions ebb, Hope floats,

I rise.

I open my eyes.

And see sacred sanctity.

About the Author

Nisha Lamichaney

Born in the hilly state of Sikkim in the year 1987, an alumni of Tashi Namgyal Academy, Gangtok, Nisha Lamichaney is an Architect by profession. She is working as a Landscape Architect in the State Government for the past six years.

Being an avid reader during her school days, she recollects being inspired by the natural setting of the environment where she grew up. Her school campus with the cherry tree in bloom and a backdrop of Mt. Kanchenjunga inspired her to write poems, which remained confined and lost in the pages of her diary.

Over the years, with the succession of events that took place in her life, she became an enthusiast in writing and her philosophy of life is evident in her writing style as well.

Her anthology "Songs of Hills" is not only her debut work but a refection of her soul.